Wedding Bells

Barbara Towell

TSL Drama

First published in Great Britain in 2017
By TSL Publications, Rickmansworth

Copyright © 1997 and 2017 Barbara Towell

ISBN / 978-1-911070-57-3
Cover image: https://pixabay.com/en/bells-church-blue-wedding-ribbon-303558/

The right of Barbara Towell to be identified as the playwright/author of this work has been asserted by the author in accordance with the UK Copyright, Designs and Patents Act 1988.

All characters and events in this publication, other than those clearly in the public domain, are fictitious and any resemblance to actual persons, living or dead, is purely coincidental.

All rights reserved. No part of this publication may be reproduced, stored in a retrieval system or transmitted, in any form or by any means without the prior written permission of the publisher, nor be otherwise circulated in any form of binding or cover other than that in which it is published and without a similar condition being imposed on the subsequent buyer.

Rights of performance

Rights of performance for this play is controlled by TSL Publications (tslbooks.uk/Drama) which issues a performing licence on payment of a fee and subject to a number of conditions (specified on tslbooks.uk/Drama). This play is fully protected under the Copyright Laws of the British Commonwealth of Nations, the United States of America and all countries of the Berne and Universal Copyright Conventions. All rights, including stage, Motion Picture, Radio, Television, Public Reading and Translation into Foreign Languages are strictly reserved. It is an infringement of the Copyright to give any performance or public reading of this play before the fee has been paid and the licence issued. The Royalty Fee is subject to contract and subject to variation at the sole discretion of TSL Publications. In Territories Overseas the fees quoted may not apply. A fee will be quoted on application to TSL Publications.

Wedding Bells

Barbara Towell

40 minutes running time

To my husband John

Wedding bells

Setting

Wedding Bells is a one act play written in the style of three connected dramatic monologues. The main action takes place in a London suburb within one day in February; this being the wedding day of Lisa and Philip.

Scenes

Scene 1 – Outside the church

Scene 2 – Inside the church

Scene 3 – Wedding reception

Scene 4 – Wedding reception

Cast
(In order of appearance.)

Marilyn — friend of the bride (age: early to mid-twenties)
Lisa — bride (age: early to mid-twenties)
Philip (Phil) — bridegroom (age: mid to end twenties)

WEDDING BELLS

Production notes
(Running time: approximately 40 minutes)

The play is written in the style of monologues, however if a director chooses, the flashbacks could be either mimed or acted out. This could be achieved by use of spotlights and a side stage. Alternatively, the character speaking steps to one side of the stage as lights fade up on the action, centre stage.

WEDDING BELLS

Props

Bench	Sc.2
Chair	Sc. 3 & 4
Table	Sc. 3,4 & 5
wine glasses with wine	Sc.3 & 4
wine bottle filled with wine	Sc.3 & 4
champagne glass – filled	Sc.5

Music & sound effects

wedding bells
organ music
sounds of crowds as typical of a buffet wedding reception

Wedding bells

Scene 1

Outside church in a London suburb

(Sound of wedding bells playing.
House lights down.
Lights up.

Enter Marilyn. She slowly wanders around the churchyard, waiting for the church to be opened. Moves to centre stage. Turns and faces audience.)

Marilyn:
God it's cold! Who in their right mind would get married in February? *(Short pause.)*
Actually, dunno really what I'm doin' 'ere – 'aven't seen them for ages? Three years – must be well over three since they moved to Nottingham.

(Pause.)

"Bin it," I says when Mum opens the family invite.
"You and Lisa go back a long time!" Mum says. "We must go – for old time sake."
Old time sake! Well, that's a laugh!
"Go on your own, Mum – you and Dad," I say. Well, that went down like a lead brick, I can tell you.

(Pause.)

Anyways, as you can see, 'ere I am. Early! Dead early. Lost the invite. *(Short pause.)*

"Definitely 12.30," Mum says. "That's another laugh. It's almost quarter to twelve and no one else in sight.
"Must take two cars!" she goes. And where's Mum's Micra? 'alfway to bloody Oxford by now, no doubt. Dad should never 'ave let her drive – always gets lost – even if it's just a blimmin' shoppin' trip to The Chimes.

(Pause.)

"But you might want to stay late – you young people, you like to burn the midnight candle," she says. Midnight candle. I ask you.

*(Marilyn walks a little way.
Sits on bench gazing at the church.)*

'ave to say, really pretty church. But why February? Better in summ … oh … Perhaps the perfect Lisa's got a little secret; one no one's tellin'?

(Pause.)

I must be mad sittin' out 'ere. No point goin' back to the car though, bloody 'eater's not workin'. Should've worn a coat instead of buyin' this thin suit I can't even afford; and now I'm freezin' as well as dreadin' the 'ole bloody thing. Well, 'ere's to 'oping at least the reception will turn out a bit of fun!

*(Pause.
Marilyn gets up and returns to centre stage. Addresses audience.)*

Anyways, Philip should've been mine by rights. This should've been *our* weddin' – 'im and me – not 'im and 'er. No way.
(Short pause.) Everyone thinks the sun shines out of her tight little bum – yeah, they do.

*(Quick fade.
Lights up.)*

"Lisa's so sweet!"
"Lisa'd give you her last penny."
"Lisa's always there when you need a friend."
Known her since Year 7, I 'ave – I'm the expert on our Lovely Lisa.

(Pause.)

"Can't you even do up your own tie?" she squeals after the first P.E. lesson at St. Finbar's.

Huh! I can see 'er now, 'ands on what she thinks are 'er sexy little 'ips – pert little smile, that pony tail swingin' – reckoned she was a sexpot even in Year 7 – and of course there were those two daft little buddies of 'ers in tow – Snotty Sarah and Nosey Norma. *(Short pause.)* Anyways, sees old battle-axe Brown stompin' down the corridor, don't she? Lovely Lisa's sneer changes into a sickly smile – and God, in a flash that Miss Goodie Two Shoes is pretendin' to 'elp me with it. Little cow.

(Pause.)

"Good to see you helping others, Lisa!" goes Miss Battle-Axe Brown, and then guess what? Scolds *me* for not 'avin' been prepared for life in secondary school. Would you believe it?
"Thank you Miss," simpers Lisa, pulling me tie so tight that I'm 'alf dead with chokin'."
"Hate that girl!" I says. Well, 'course not out loud.

(Pause.)

Then, you know what? 'Cos our surnames both start with "S", don't we end up sittin' next to each other in nearly every blimmin' lesson? On top of that, as sod's law would 'ave it, it turns out that our mums know each other from the 'airdresser's – and jeeez we almost live round the corner from each other! I guess, that's 'ow after a bit we got to be – well, sort of – friends.

And before I knows it – she's actually goin' round tellin' everyone that we're best mates ... Yeah, best mates when I lets her copy my Maths 'omework! Or buys 'er a load of sweets and chocolate bars. Best mates? –
Fun-ny. Only best mates when 'er cool gang aren't around.

*(Marilyn shivers and hugs herself.
Stands.)*

Sod this for a laugh, I'm goin' back to the car ... Oh! There's the vicar. Yip, I think 'e's goin' to open up.

(Marilyn walks towards side of stage. Turns as if speaking to the vicar.)

Mornin' Vicar ... Yes, I know I'm extremely early. Better than bein' late though, ay? ... Um, cold, but sunny ... *(Marilyn sighs.)* Yeh Vicar, they'll make a ... a lovely couple.

(Lights down.)

Scene 2

Inside church

(Lights up.

Marilyn enters. Walks for a while looking round church. Then walks to centre stage and sits on the pew, facing audience.)

Marilyn:
These benches, pews, whatever you call 'em, they're blimmin' hard. Numb the bum as well as freeze it rigid. *(Short pause.)* Jeez! There 'e is, Philip, with 'is best man. Well, guess e's the best man. *(Looks down.)* Head down.

(Pause.)

Yeah, Philip you should 'ave been mine. If there was any bloody justice in this world, you should 'ave been mine. Justice – now that's a laugh. I saw you first. Love at first sight it was when I saw you there, proppin' up the bar. Saw you every Tuesday and Thursday after that – down at the Coach and 'orses.

(Pause.
Quick fade.
Lights up.)

"Go on, Go and talk to him," Lisa says urgin' me on when we meet at Mcdonalds. "Bump into him accidentally on purpose – you know what I mean – that's if you really can't pluck up the courage to go over and say hi, or something and be all friendly like."

She then says while sprayin' 'er wrist with 'er favourite scent Charlie – as if she thinks I'm about twelve years old: "God! We *are* living in the 21st century, Marilyn, not in Victorian times."
"But, I'm not sure if 'e'll like me," I says.
Now, even to myself I'm soundin' like a twelve year old – twelve goin' on eleven.
"Don't be ridiculous, of course he will," she says. "You've got quite nice blonde hair – even if it is out of a bottle – and, not a bad figure – 'specially when you're wearing those loose jeans."
She's dead unconvincin'. And dead 'orrible when you think about it.

(Pause.)

Ooh God! These knickers are so blimmin' tight. Should 'ave bought size 14. Bin eatin' too many of them cakes instead of sellin' them. Definitely left the bloody diet too late. Late, like everythin' ... except bein' early for this damn weddin'.

(Sounds of footsteps.)

Who's this lot comin' up the aisle? – Is it Mum and ...? *(Sounds disappointed.)* No.
Oh God! It's nosey Norma. 'aven't seen her in ages. Put on more than a few pounds, I see.

(Pause.)

Hi, Norma ... No. No one sittin' this side.

(Marilyn points to vacant place on one side of her.)

Nice to meet you ... Sid, did you say? Your fiancé, Norma? ... Oh lovely ... No, I'm in between guys actually. *(Aside.)* That's a laugh. Can't remember when I last 'ad a date – and God knows when there'll be a next ... What's that Norma? ... Yes, love the stained-glass windows too ... No, no, you're right, can't beat a church weddin'.

*(Pause.
Marilyn addresses audience.)*

Anyway, gettin' back to The Coach and 'orses. There was this do on for Valentine's Day.

*(Quick fade.
Lights up.)*

"Well, there's your chance, a Valentine's do!" Lisa says. You know, like she's a real mate and wants to do me a good turn. Then she goes, "We'll meet at 8.00 outside the pub. Don't go in without me though. I don't like going into pubs on my own." Like hell she doesn't!
And guess whose still 'angin' outside the Coach and 'orses – just like a lemon, at 'alf past 8? Well, it wasn't Lisa. So there I am – scroungin' a ciggy – or two ... And I don't even smoke!!
After a bit I think, she can't be comin' – I'll just go 'ome. Then I think, no don't be such a wimp girl and make meself go in. *(Pause.)* And there she is – well, she certainly 'ad the courage to go in on 'er own, did Lovely Lisa. And not only that – she's already sniffed 'im out, my Philip – and she's right close to 'im, sippin' 'er white wine all prizzy like. Surprise, surprise! – and there's 'im, lookin' at 'er – like a bloody Tom cat on 'eat. When she turns she sees me – and believe it or not, doesn't look even a bit guilty. She calls, "Hi Marilyn – then she introduces 'im to me – "This is Marilyn – Marilyn Monroe ..." and then they're both in fits of laughter. And there am I feelin' a worse lemon than when I was standin' out there freezin' alive.

(Marilyn turns from audience and looks as if to Don the best man.)

'ope I can keep up all this smilin'. Guess he must be Philip's brother, the best man – looks like 'im. Not as good lookin' though. But won't be turnin' 'im down if 'e asks me for a dance later. Better not tempt prov ... no prova ... – provanence – Oh whatever, ay?

*(Quick fade.
Lights up.)*

"Did you get any Valentine cards, Marilyn?" she asks me.
"Got one," I lie, not to feel a prat.
She then laughs looking straight at Philip – and says, "Always gets one from her mum, Phil!"
She's already callin' him Phil. Phil in that intimate smarmy way – just like that Beverley in the repeat of *Abigail's Party* I saw on telly. Anyways, no prizes for guessin' 'ow long I stayed after that!

(Pause.)

Well, I couldn't believe it when next day I get this text.

As u went so soon. Took it u gone off P. So got date with him. Hope it's okay.

Well, no it was not bloody okay! But what could I do?

(Pause.)

Funny, now when I think about it – 'ow I caught up with Philip at Lisa's party. Don't think she even remembered that I'd fancied 'im first. *(Short pause.)* You know what parties are like? Lots of drink et cetera, et cetera. Thought 'e was interested in me for a while. That was a laugh – yeah. Well, a laugh for 'im. Both a bit drunk, I guess. "It was nothing," 'e said later ... but it **was** somethin' to me.

(Organ music starts to play in background.)

Oh God! The organ's strikin' up. And no Mum and Dad yet. Typical ... Oh Philip's looking round now – anxious to see the Lovely Lisa, no doubt – ignoring me of course. Thank God they live in Nottingham.

(Pause. Organ music continues to play.)

Jeez, thank 'eavens, Mum, Dad ... at last they're 'ere. Come on. *(Marilyn beckons.)* Over 'ere. Good, they've seen me.

(Pause.)

(Marilyn whispers.) Hi Mum! Took the wrong exit? ... Well, you're all 'ere now that's the main thing. ... Okay Dad, but I did say you should drive. ... I know ... I know what she's like ... And hi my little guy. Enjoyed your sleepover at Nana's and Grandad's? ... Good. Yeh, I know you always do. Quickly, come and sit next to Mummy.
(Turns her head, looking to her other side.)
Yes, Norma, my son – and yeah, 'e does look amazin'ly like Philip, don't 'e?

(Organ plays 'The Wedding March'.)

Sit still now, Phil. The bride's just arrived.

(Marilyn as if patting her son Phil on the head, turns and addresses audience after a short pause.)

Can't wait to introduce 'im to the bride and groom at the reception. I'm sure they will be so pleased to meet 'im. A surprise weddin' gift for Philip – and of course, the Lovely Lisa.
(Marilyn smiles.)

(Lights down.)

Wedding bells

Scene 3

Wedding reception

(Sounds of people talking and laughing at wedding reception. Lights up.

Enter Lisa with glass in hand. She walks to front stage which is slightly off-centre and addresses audience.)

Lisa:
She's a sly one all right! Kid! *(Short pause.)* Huh! I wonder why Mum never mentioned Marilyn's got a kid? Now, I know why she never replied to my texts – or phone calls for that matter – the *real* reason. To be quite honest, I'd always thought it was – was because she felt such an idiot after my party – pushing herself at Phil like that. *(Lisa walks to centre stage and sits on chair.)*

*(Quick fade.
Lights fade up.)*

"Marilyn?" Phil said to me at that party, after I'd seen them coming out of the spare bedroom together – "Marilyn? – me and her? – I was just helping her find her anorak. You are joking, aren't you? Marilyn Monroe *she is not*," he said with a chuckle. Then gave me a very convincing kiss. And I believed him! Taken in, hook, line and sinker – I'll kill him. I'll kill him, I *will*.

(Pause.)

Yes, that's right, keep smiling Philip my lad – for now. But just you wait. Just you wait until I get you alone in that hotel bedroom – and you'll see what you get. And I can guarantee, absolutely guarantee it won't be what you're expecting!

(Lisa walks across to a table laid with food.
Picks up a chicken leg. Puts it down without eating it.
Pours another glass of wine and takes a large sip before returning to the chair and sits.)

God, I've quite lost my appetite. *(Short pause.)* The thought of ... I suppose she was jealous, mad with me deep down. *(Pause.)* She always was a contrary one. The jealous type. At school, she never liked it when I had other friends. A real hanger-on then – and a real hanger-on when we left school. Don't even know why I bothered with the fat tart! *(Drinks wine from glass.)* That's it. That – is – it! She became a habit – the Marilyn habit. What a bad habit she was. So beware Marilyn, bad habits don't end well.

(Lisa trying to pull herself together, gets up. Wanders around for a few moments smiling and miming brief conversation with guests before returning to chair.
Sits, facing audience.)

Honestly, to be so angry with me! After me, going to all that trouble to introduce her to Phil. Have to admit I didn't know he'd turn out to be such a catch. But hey, what does *she* do? Chickens out within minutes! So, what was I to do when Phil asked me for a date? Hey, what would you have done in my position?

(Pause.)

I don't know why Mum was so insistent. So what? They see each other at the hairdresser's every so often. I see the postman every day, doesn't mean I have to invite him to my wedding, does it?

(Quick fade.
Lights fade up.)

"Oh! But Lisa, we've known the Shaws for donkeys' years. What with them living so nearby, it could be really quite embarrassing," says Mum over and over – and over again.
But Marilyn? Why Marilyn too? I haven't spoken or heard from her for ages.

(Pause.)

As you can plainly see, eventually I gave in – but put the Shaws right at the bottom of the reserve list. And what do you know? As fortune – or more to the point, misfortune would have it – they of course, end up coming! Plus the kid – uninvited, I might point out.
"Doesn't eat much. Can have a bite of mine," says Marilyn smiling as *her* Phil shakes hands with *my* Phil.

(Quick fade.
Lights fade up.)

I simply could not believe my eyes when she introduced *him*.
"Congrats!" she says in that sugary, high pitched voice. "Meet me son – Phil."
Then she says to the kid, emphasising *Phil:* "Shake hands with Philip – and Lisa, *Phil.*"
All the time her eyes are darting from me to my Phil. You don't have to be a mind reader to know what's going on in her conniving little brain!
Well, I stood there itching to slap her face. Her silly, stupid, common little face. Just itching, I was. Wanted to take that smirk right off it! *(Short pause.)* Then I picture the scene; me slapping her – her slapping me, Phil slapping us both. And then I see the guests' faces ... and a voice inside me whispers, "Don't let that nasty little bitch ruin everything."
And you know what? I am **not** going to let her ruin my big day – and certainly ... absolutely **not** going to let her ruin my marriage. No way! I will not give her the satisfaction*!*

(Sips wine from the glass.
Gets up from the chair and walks to the very front of the stage.
Continues to address audience.)

Now, strange as it may seem to any normal person, Phil – that is, my Phil – doesn't seem to have noticed. – Well, he's noticed the kid of course – but not that it's the spitting image of him. *(Short pause.)*
Honestly, Phil simply didn't blink an eye – just shook hands with little Phil, and made some unfunny joke about them sharing the same name.

(Pause.)

When you think about it *(Looks at women in audience.)* – men aren't like us girls – perceptive – are they? Well, maybe in this case, it's lucky. But what's really, *really* lucky; is that my Phil and I will be far away from here by morning – off to the Caribbean – and once the honeymoon is over, safely back in Nottingham. With no Marilyn – and definitely no mini Phil – ever!

(Lights down.)

Scene 4

Wedding reception

(Sounds of people talking and laughing at a wedding reception. Lights up.)

Philip is sitting at a table facing the audience. A glass and bottle of wine is in front of him. He stares ahead. Suddenly aware of the audience, he begins to speak.)

Philip:
You expect surprises on your wedding day, don't you? Lots of them – nice surprises, that is. But not shocks. Certainly not a shock like meeting your own son for the first time – one you never even knew existed. Quite frankly, that's no shock. That's a nightmare. The sort of nightmare which leaves you reeling; feeling more than a little sick when you wake up. In fact, a bloody bombshell. You know the kind?

(Pause.)

Lisa hasn't said anything. Amazing as it might seem, I actually don't think she's noticed the likeness. More worried about her dress, her hair, her make-up, I guess. Women are bound to be like that on their big day, aren't they? What with the photographs and everything. *(Short pause.)* Any rate, she's still smiling; and I'm still smiling. In fact, thank God, everyone's still smiling. And let's hope we can keep it that way.

(Picks up a wine glass and gulps down quite a lot of wine. Puts the glass down and continues to speak.)

Talking of photographs, to be frank, I probably only noticed the likeness between me and the lad because of that photo in Mum's bedroom. The one on her bedside cabinet. The one of me at about three. Me, wearing those daft shorts with the flappy long legs and my faithful Superman T-shirt ... Me ... *(Sighs.)* about the same age as Marilyn's Phil... Marilyn and m ... my Phil ... looking cheeky ... like ... my *son*. Oh God*!*

(Gulps down wine from wine glass.
Refills it from bottle on the table.)

But Lisa won't have seen the photo. No. She never goes in Mum's bedroom. Why would she? *(Short pause.)* Strange when you think about it. In fact quite ironic. Walk up the aisle a single guy, no cares in the world – there I am repeating the vows – and to be honest, not really thinking much about what the words mean.
"Are you ready to accept children lovingly from God?" asks the vicar.
"I am," I reply in blissful ignorance. For hey presto! Minutes later, as if by magic, I'm a dad! Imagine it.

(Picks up glass of wine.
Before taking a sip Philip puts down the glass.
Stands up and walks to front of centre stage and addresses audience again.)

Now Marilyn, she's a dark horse. Fancy having that lad – and not even telling me? I mean he's a chip off the old block and no mistake. The mind boggles, it really does. Don't know whether I should be angry ... angry or relieved? Quite frankly ... I'm ... I'm mystified. *(Short pause.)* Perhaps, if I'm honest, I *am* relieved. Relieved I never knew. *(Short pause.)* Though he does look a pretty nice kid. Well, not pretty of course, he's a boy. But nice. Cute ... in a manly sort of way.

(Philip walks back and sits on chair.)

Never thought about Marilyn after Lisa's party – well, after that phone call. Pushed her right out of my mind.

*(Quick fade.
Lights fade up.)*

It was a Friday. Yes, a Friday when she caught up with me – more or less a week on from Lisa's awful party.
I remember it had been a really busy week at work, what with Tom being on holiday and me having to deal with lets as well as sales; and I just couldn't wait for the weekend – to spend time with Lisa now we'd got over that bad patch. *(Short pause.)* I'd just had a shower and was leaving to pick her up for a Chinese meal, when the phone rang. Thought it was Lisa at first, changing her mind, wanting to go to that new expensive Italian place she'd been on about. *(Short pause.)* "When are we going to have that drink then?" It was Marilyn.
"What drink?" I said. Of course I knew what drink, but I was playing innocent.

(Pause.)

Now don't get me wrong, I'm not proud of what I did. In fact, looking back, I'm quite ashamed really. I want you to know that. But it was a while ago. And I was still young. You know, a tad immature. Any rate, haven't we all done things we're not proud of some time or another?

(Pause.)

I don't know what you're talking about, Marilyn," I remember saying.
Marilyn's chirpy tone was no longer chirpy. It now resembled that of a high pitched squawky parrot.
"I don't know what you're talking about," I repeated.

(Pause.)

Anyway, back to Lisa's party. I know it's not an excuse, but the thing was, Lisa had been in a mood all day. You wouldn't have thought it was a party she was preparing. No, you'd think it was some kind of majorly important reception designed to impress the new boss at her office. God the way she was carrying on!

(Short pause.)

Disaster! Her mum hadn't vacuumed the floor before she'd had gone off to Brighton for the weekend. Guess who was greeted with the hoover when they arrived? Next, I was in the dog house for having forgotten to buy the booze and extra snacky things, as she calls them.
"For God sake, Phil," she kept saying, pulling away when I wanted a cuddle. "Is that all you think about? There's so much to do."
Well, vacuuming was not what I'd had in mind while her parents were away, that's for sure. *(Short pause.)* I remember thinking they were probably having more of a dirty weekend – a lot more fun than we were having! Yes, and not to forget the Chelsea match I was missing. Vacuuming didn't seem much of a substitute for football somehow. *(Short pause.)* Half an hour before the guests were due – literally everything was ready. Perfect. That's what I thought ... and definitely enough time for what I had in mind. *(Short pause.)* Well, we'd hardly got started when I'm hearing: "You're spoiling my make-up. Get off Phil."

(Pause.)

But to be frank what really, really annoyed me ... got under my skin ... was the way she changed once that front door opened and the guests appeared. Bubbly and all gushing smiles. And no miserable scowls for that ex of hers, Paul. You know what? She didn't even bother introducing me, just started fluttering her eye lashes and flirting. Not really like my Lisa at all, to be honest. And yes, I was surprised; 'specially as she'd always told me Paul had bored her to tears. *(Short pause.)* Now, don't get me wrong, Lisa and I get on – we've always got on – like a house on fire. Like peas in a pod, her mum says. Otherwise there wouldn't be this wedding, would there? Looking back, I suppose I was reading more into it than there really was.

(Fills up glass and gulps down wine in one go.)

Look, to cut a long story short, the evening went like this. There was Marilyn. Not bad looking – generously built in all the right places, if you know what I mean. *(Winks. Short pause.)* "Hi!" she said coming up to me while I was pouring myself another beer. Anyway, we chatted a while. And very friendly she was too. Men can sense when a woman fancies them, can't they? But I didn't do anything. No. Not at first that is. Just drifted off, got a few shots of scotch from the drinks' cabinet. Knew Lisa's dad wouldn't mind. Actually, that evening I really didn't care one way or another whether he did or not.

(Pause.)

It was about half an hour later that I caught up with Marilyn again – on the landing. She was coming out of the spare bedroom, holding her anorak. "Going already?" I asked. "Why don't you stay a bit longer? It's still early." Well, before I knew it we were kissing. *(Pause.)* Things were going well. It was only once we were inside the spare room, heading for more than a kiss and a cuddle that she broke away, and suddenly got all indignant, asking if I thought she was *that* kind of girl. The kind who has one night stands ... especially with a mate's boyfriend. Confused messages ay? – I'll say.

(Drinks from wine glass.)

It was then I told the great big porky – that I'd always secretly liked her, found her drop-dead gorgeous. To be fair she had led me on. But anyway, she needed a bit more convincing than that, so I ended up promising it wasn't a one off – I'd ring her – go for a drink – soon. Now that worked a treat. *(Short pause.)* Afterwards, lying with her amongst those coats on the bed, it dawned on me what I'd done and regretted it, regretted it big time. *(Short pause.)* And even more so later when Lisa spotted us coming out of the spare bedroom. Bloody hell, my heart took an extra beat or ten, I can tell you.

"Marilyn and me?" I said to a tearful Lisa. Even I was surprised how convincing I sounded. "You must be joking." And for good measure, added: "Marilyn Monroe, she is not." Thankfully, Lisa began to giggle. Phew! Considering my mind was a cloud of alcohol, I think I managed that pretty well, don't you?

(Stands and wanders around stage for a few seconds before returning to chair.)

But I must admit the way I handled Marilyn's phone call the following week ... well, it was definitely not my finest hour.
"It was nothing ..." I repeated, putting down the receiver. And then decided to treat Lisa to that expensive Italian bistro. *(Short pause.)* In truth, I never spared Marilyn another thought – that is until today ... my wedding day, when it turns out to be **something** after all. *(Short pause.)* My God, me, I'm a dad.

(Quick fade.
Lights fade up.

Philip stands. He pulls the knot of his tie and straightens the flower on his lapel as if to smarten up.)

Come on, pull yourself together, lad. *(Smiles at the guests.)* Today's not the time for all this. Smile. Keep on smiling at Lisa; and concentrate on enjoying, what after all, is a bloody expensive wedding – and don't forget the "cuddles" and champers awaiting you in that posh bridal suite later on.

(Wanders around stage. Smiling and miming brief exchanges of conversation with guests.
Returns to chair and sits.)

Lisa's looking more relaxed now, thank God. With a bit of luck, she'll be smiling even more once I've made my speech. Think I'll give some of those jokes a miss though — yes, compliment her more instead.

(Picks up glass and drinks.)

Yes, ignorance is bliss. Keeps everyone happy. Yep, there's plenty of time after the honeymoon to get to know my son. *(Short pause.)* A blessing now I think of it, that Lisa has never hit it off with Mum. So it shouldn't be too difficult to take trips down south — on my own — to visit "her". *(Short pause.)* Um, but what about Marilyn? *(Short pause.)* Well, I feel sure the promise of some financial help will ensure she keeps schtum.

(Smiling, drinks from the wine glass.)

Yes, best not to rock the boat. Best not to upset the apple-cart so to speak — live in wedded bliss. Best Lisa doesn't know little Phil's my son, don't you think?

(Lights down.)

VOICE OVER (male): I think we all agree that this has been a most joyful occasion. So please be upstanding and raise your glasses for the bride and groom. The toast is — the happy couple.

(Sounds of wedding bells.)